Dear Parent:

Congratulations! Your child is taking the first steps on an exciting journey. The destination? Independent reading!

STEP INTO READING® will help your child get there. The program offers books at five levels that accompany children from their first attempts at reading to reading success. Each step includes fun stories, fiction and nonfiction, and colorful art. There are also Step into Reading Sticker Books, Step into Reading Math Readers, and Step into Reading Phonics Readers— a complete literacy program with something to interest every child.

Learning to Read, Step by Step!

Ready to Read Preschool–Kindergarten
• big type and easy words • rhyme and rhythm • picture clues
For children who know the alphabet and are eager to begin reading.

Reading with Help Preschool–Grade 1
• basic vocabulary • short sentences • simple stories
For children who recognize familiar words and sound out new words with help.

Reading on Your Own Grades 1–3
• engaging characters • easy-to-follow plots • popular topics
For children who are ready to read on their own.

Reading Paragraphs Grades 2–3
• challenging vocabulary • short paragraphs • exciting stories
For newly independent readers who read simple sentences with confidence.

Ready for Chapters Grades 2–4
• chapters • longer paragraphs • full-color art
For children who want to take the plunge into chapter books but still like colorful pictures.

STEP INTO READING® is designed to give every child a successful reading experience. The grade levels are only guides. Children can progress through the steps at their own speed, developing confidence in their reading, no matter what their grade.

Remember, a lifetime love of reading starts with a single step!

www.stepintoreading.com
www.seussville.com
www.catinthehat.com

Educators and librarians, for a variety of teaching tools, visit us at
www.randomhouse.com/teachers

Library of Congress Cataloging-in-Publication Data
Krensky, Stephen.
Do not open this crate! / by Stephen Krensky ; illustrated by Aristides Ruiz.
   p.   cm. — (Step into reading. A step 4 book)
Based on the motion picture screenplay written by Alec Berg & David Mandel & Jeff Schaffer, based on the book by Dr. Seuss.
SUMMARY: A visit from a very big cat in a very big hat creates so much excitement that Sally and Conrad forget all about being bored.
ISBN 0-375-82488-X (trade) — ISBN 0-375-92488-4 (lib. bdg.)
[1. Cats—Fiction.   2. Imagination—Fiction.]
I. Ruiz, Aristides, ill.   II. Seuss, Dr. Cat in the hat.   III. Title.
IV. Series: Step into reading. Step 4 book.
PZ7.K883Do   2003   [E]—dc21   2002154249

Printed in the United States of America   10 9 8 7 6 5 4 3 2 1

By Stephen Krensky

Illustrated by Aristides Ruiz

Based on the motion picture screenplay
written by
Alec Berg & David Mandel & Jeff Schaffer

Based on the book by Dr. Seuss

Random House 🏠 New York

Chapter 1

Bored, bored, bored. Conrad and Sally were bored.

"Stop picking on me!" said Sally.

"I can't help it," said Conrad. "There's nothing else to do and no one else to pick on."

"Except me," said a strange voice.

Both children jumped. Who said that?

A figure came in through the doorway. Conrad stared. He had never seen such a big cat. Or such a big hat.

"Since your sitter's asleep and your mom is away, I came here for fun," said the Cat. "So let's play."

"You came to the wrong house," Conrad told him. "There's no fun here."

6

The Cat tapped his hat. A doctor's headlamp popped out.

"Say *ahhh!*" he told Conrad. Then he looked down his throat.

"I see the problem," said the Cat. "You have a case of the Worst-Day-Evers. Fresh out of imagination. But I can fix that!"

The Cat ran out the front door.
He came back with a very big crate.
"What's *that*?" asked Sally.
"A jack-in-the-box?"

He opened the lid. Out sprang
Thing One and Thing Two.

"It's more of a 'Thing-in-a-box,'"
said the Cat. "Nobody's bored once
these two pop out!"

"Oh, yeah?" said Conrad. "What is
it they do?"

"Wait and see," said the Cat. "Are
you ready, Thing One? Thing Two?"

Chapter 2

Thing One was ready. He picked up the closest object and threw it to Thing Two.

Thing Two threw it back.

Sally liked to play catch. And she would have played, too—but they were throwing Mom's best vase!

"Stop that!" she cried.

She ran from Thing One to Thing Two. Then from Thing Two to Thing One. But she could not catch the vase.

The Cat slapped his knee. "Hot dog!" he said. "A game of keep-away."

Conrad didn't want to play
keep-away—or help his sister. He
wanted to look inside the crate.

He knelt on the floor. Then he lifted
the lid. A strange ooze seeped out.

The ooze slid across the floor, then curled around a chair. The chair's legs wobbled.

POP! POP! POP! POP!

The legs had grown feet. Big pink feet. Conrad was amazed.

What would happen next? he wondered. Conrad couldn't wait to see.

BAM!

The Cat slammed the crate's lid down.

The ooze disappeared—and so did the feet. Now the chair was just a chair again.

"Why did you do that?" Conrad asked the Cat.

"This crate is no toy!" said the Cat. "It's a doorway between my world and yours. And that door must stay shut. So whatever you do—DO NOT OPEN THIS CRATE!"

Just to make sure, the Cat snapped on a crab lock and slapped on a warning.

Chapter 3

Conrad did not like locks—or warnings.
So when the Cat turned away, he crept
back to the crate.

He pulled out a paper clip. Then he
knelt down to work.

Back and forth he turned the clip. This
way and that. It tickled the crab lock's
stomach. The crab giggled. Then—*click!*—
the lock opened.

Conrad reached to lift the lid and—
"No, don't!" cried his sister.

Conrad froze. Was Sally
talking to him? He turned to look.
Whew! It was just that stupid
keep-away game. Thing One threw the
vase right out the window—and Conrad's
dog, Nevins, jumped out after it!

17

Sally ran to the window. The vase lay on the ground in a hundred pieces! "Mom will never forgive us!" she cried.

Nevins barked.

"It's all right, Nevins," Sally said. "It's not your fault. Come back in."

But Nevins didn't come back in.

Instead, Nevins ran this way and that way. Then he ran right out of the yard.

Conrad raced to the window. "Nevins, come back!" he shouted.

But Nevins was gone.

"And that's a doggone shame," said the Cat.

"We have to catch him!" said Conrad.

"Agreed," said the Cat. So he opened the back door and led the chase.

Sally followed. So did Conrad, forgetting all about the unlocked crate behind him.

Chapter 4

When Conrad, Sally, and the Cat returned with Nevins, they all stood in the doorway and stared.

The house looked different. *Very* different. In fact, thought the Cat, it looked an awful lot like the inside of his crate.

"What happened?" cried Sally.

The Cat frowned at Conrad. "My crate *is* still locked. Isn't it?" he asked.

Conrad turned bright red. "I picked the lock," he confessed.

"Oh, brother," said Sally. "We're in real trouble now."

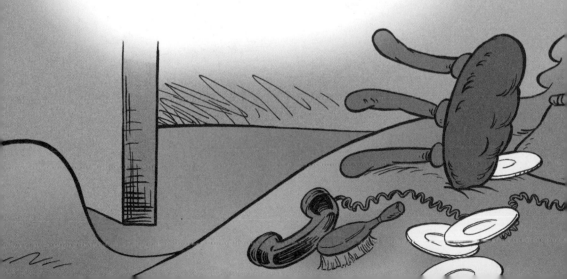

Very carefully they walked into the house. The hall carpet hung like a rope bridge in midair.

Below them, book birds flew by. The floor rippled and rolled in orange waves.

Sally sneezed. The carpet bridge swayed and swung. They nearly fell off!

"Okay, I messed up," Conrad told the Cat. "Now, how do I fix it?"

"Simple," said the Cat. "We find the crate you opened—and WE SHUT IT!"

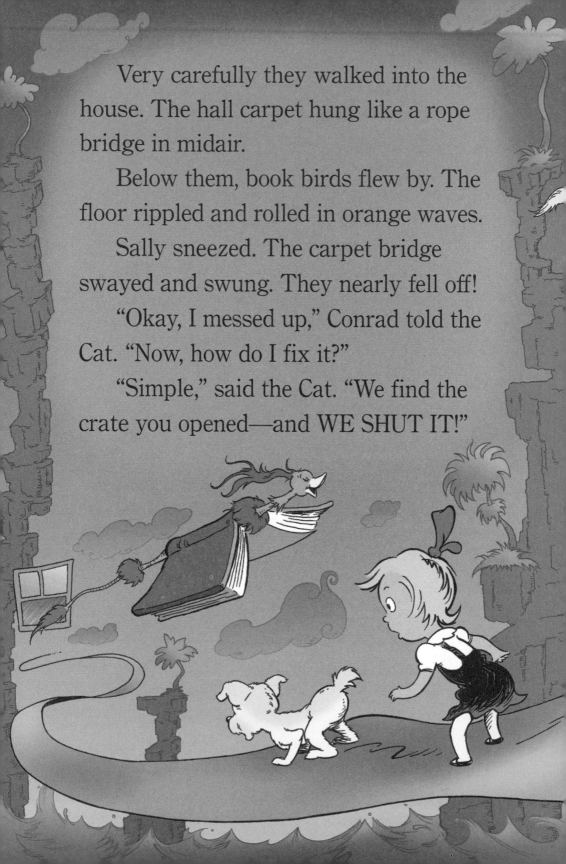

They moved toward the living room. "Holy cow!" gasped Conrad.

The chairs, tables, and sofa were *huge*. The walls moved in and out as if they were breathing. And they could barely see the ceiling.

"There's the crate!" cried Conrad.

In the corner, the crate was rocking back and forth. Gooey ooze dribbled down the sides. Its lid was wide open.

Sally made them stop.

"I hear someone yelling," she said.

DO NOT OPEN THIS CRATE!

Chapter 5

"What's going on over here?" yelled Lawrence Quinn at the front door. "I heard noises!"

Conrad bit his lip. Mr. Quinn was their neighbor. He didn't like kids. And yelling was his favorite sport.

Mr. Quinn took one look at the house and blew his top.

"Look at this place!" he yelled. "I'm going to call your mother right now. Where's your phone?"

Mr. Quinn ran onto the swaying carpet
bridge—and slipped right off.

"I'll be baaaaaack!" he shouted.

"Wow. That was a long way down,"
said Conrad.

"Come on!" said Sally. "The crate!"

Just then, something rose up from inside the crate. Up, up, up it went. Larger and larger it grew until it towered over them like a giant parade balloon.

"Uh-oh!" said Sally.

It was Mr. Quinn, only now he was twenty feet tall!

Sally tried to run. But the giant Quinn grabbed her. "Where do you think *you're* going?" he roared.

"Conrad!" cried Sally. "Help!"

DO NOT OPEN THIS CRATE!

Chapter 6

Conrad had to fight the giant Quinn. But how?

He noticed a flashlight nearby and reached for it. But Quinn grabbed it first. "Is this what you wanted?" said Quinn. "It's just a stupid flashlight."

He tossed it back to Conrad and laughed.

"A word of advice," said the Cat. "Get some imagination. Fast."

Imagination? Conrad wondered what the Cat meant. Then he knew!

If the Cat's magic crate could change the whole house, maybe it could change other things, too.

"*Just* a flashlight?" Conrad said. He flipped on the beam. "Or is it a baseball bat?"

At that, the beam took the shape of a giant baseball bat. Conrad swung. The beam whacked Quinn in the leg.

"Owwwww!" Quinn cried out, and dropped Sally.

Sally fell
through
the air.
"AAAIIIIIEEEEE!"
she screamed.

Conrad bounced onto the
sofa and sprang up to grab her.
"Your ride is here," he told her.

He clicked on the flashlight.
The beam became a fire pole.
Down they slid to safety!

"That's it!" Quinn yelled. "No more Mister Nice Guy!"

Better think fast! Conrad told himself. He saw a painting on the wall and grabbed it. "All aboooooard!" he shouted.

The train in the painting roared right out of the frame. It headed straight for Quinn and scooped him up. Then it chugged right back into the painting.

"Next stop—next door. And that's where you belong," said Conrad.

He hung the painting back on the wall.

The Cat smiled and said, "Well, that certainly shows you the danger of having a one-track mind!"

Chapter 7

"Let's hurry up and shut that crate," Sally told Conrad. "Mom will be home soon."

They each grabbed one end of the crate's lid.

"One, two, three—" said Conrad.

"Close it!" said Sally.

Together they slammed the lid down tight. Then Conrad clicked the lock.

"Stand back!" said the Cat.

Suddenly a great roar filled the air. A big funnel cloud rose up. It grabbed chairs, tables, lamps, and books.

Everything started flying over their heads!

Finally the funnel was sucked back
into the crate. It rattled one last time. Then
everything was still.

"Wow! Everything is back to normal," said Sally. Then she pointed to the coffee table. "Even Mom's vase!"

The broken vase was fixed. It looked as good as new.

"Hold your applause," said the Cat. "I'm a shy guy."

The Cat saw Thing One and Thing Two. They were peeking in from around a corner.

"The coast is clear," he called to them. "Come on out. It's time to go."

"Where are you going?" asked Sally.

"My work here is done," said the Cat. "Unless you two are still bored. Because if you are, I'll just open the crate again—"

Conrad looked at Sally. "NO WAY!" they said together.

Then Thing One and Thing Two lifted the crate and carried it out.

"Oh, and Conrad," said the Cat, "just remember one thing. The next time you want to unlock a crate that says DO NOT OPEN—"

"Yes?" said Conrad.

"I may not be here to help."

"I'll remember," promised Conrad.

"And if he doesn't remember," said Sally, "I'll remind him."

"Good," said the Cat.

Then he tipped his tall hat and he waved a good-bye. And Conrad and Sally breathed a very big sigh.